Tales of a Traveler

Guy Breshears

Published by Guy Breshears

Cover photo: A Boeing 747 on final approach to Hong Kong International Airport. March 29, 2013. Photo by author, © 2013. All rights reserved.

First Printing: 2019

ISBN 978-988-77039-3-8

Other books by the author:
Loyal till Death: A Diary of the 13th New York Artillery
Major Granville Haller: Dismissed with Malice
To Seize Their Lands: Manifest Destiny in Washington State
Visit http://www.heritagebooks.com for more information of these books

Of Papers and Protests: Hong Kong responds to Occupy Central, volumes 1, 2 and 3
Visit http://www.lulu.com/spotlight/gbreshears for more information about these books

For more information about this book contact the publisher:

Breshears, Guy
PO Box 88409
Sham Shui Po Post Office
Kowloon
Hong Kong

Dedication

To my wife who has stood by me ever since I have arrived in Hong Kong. I could not have survived without her continuing support.

Also, to Our Lady of China: May all that reflect on this book be filled with guidance in their journeys in life. Finally, pray for the faithful who live here and have recourse to thee in these difficult times.

Table of Stories

THE BRAVE BUNNY

PROLOGUE

Inland and beyond the northern European coast and far from where I write this tale there lays a once mighty castle in ruins and not much remains standing. Many say it's the legendary Aldermount while others deny and scoff at this; they make the claim that it is the original location of the castle Fairwinds (or some long-forgotten one). They also claim that Aldermount is just a myth and a story for fools, romantics, and adventurers. There is nothing there to give claim to either side so readers, and visitors, are free to believe whatever they want.

However, it seems odd to be the original Fairwinds castle as it is so far from the coast and where the famous Fairwinds castle stands. If true, then perhaps it once held a different name that has been lost to antiquity. For nothing has been found stating a different name or location for Fairwinds but not all records have been recorded or have been lost.

It is possible that this is a long-forgotten castle but I cannot find anything that supports this claim. I have searched over a large amount of documents, far and near, and found nothing to give credit to this conjecture. But, perhaps it may be true without further evidence or allegation.

I, for one, will not judge you if you believe if this is the legendary Aldermount or not.

In this decaying castle most of the fortress walls remain standing, though many have crumbled because of time and weather and who knows what else; the main gate, with the arch, are always opened for the gates have fallen off and disappeared somewhere into the annals of time. Beyond the walls the once supposed majestic buildings and living quarters have also fallen. Only outlines or crumbled walls can be seen.

Most castle ruins, like Fairwinds, are well known and have many people visit them. However, Aldermount seems to be the exception and not many visit this place, except perhaps thrill seekers, adventures, the curious, and ghost hunters. Hushed rumors abound from those that do visit there, and the stories are all about the same. An odd feeling, it is often stated but always undefined and hard to put into words, that something is there and watching over the castle making sure nothing grows and nothing is disturbed.

The only thing that seems to grow, and grows quite well, is a bush in the middle of what was once the main courtyard. It is near the old well that was used as the marker for the town square when Aldermount was first built. Here, visitors who brave the eerie feelings of the castle report they find a sense of relaxation and a sense of purpose. However, those that try to take a cutting of the bush often meet, later, with lingering illness and a deep depression. When the bush cutting is taken back to the ruined castle (for those who are brave enough to try) the person with the illness recovers and tell of visions of a warning that no one is to take a cutting for it is to be there as a memorial forever. But none can tell for whom exactly the memorial is for.

Within a few hours walking there is a dense forest that even fewer visits. Those that manage to survive entering deeply into the forest babble on about something no one can quite understand. These poor suffering souls never fully recover and mention that there is a statue (but again can never fully describe it) that is so holy, so sacred that those who dared to view the statue are struck with a sense of unworthiness that stays with them for the rest of their lives.

On maps it is indeed listed as the Aldermount forest. Perhaps because the city of Fairwinds have given up with whatever name they gave it and listed it according to petitions and legends. Or perhaps it really is the Aldermount forest of lore.

My interest in this story started when I was a young boy. My father and I often went on trips to explore new places. Every summer I looked forward to these trips with him. We both enjoyed the time together and got to see large parts of the world that most would only dream of.

One year was to the castle for we had both read and heard stories about it and really wanted to see it for ourselves. Over my school year we talked and planned most of our trip and gathered up all the information we could.

On the actual trip we managed to park the car, get out and walk to the main gate entrance. From there we were able to peer in to see the green, growing bush in the distance. But that was all we were able to do for we both didn't feel like going in and exploring more. We looked at the courtyard for what seemed like hours and walked around the outside of the main wall. We then left and never returned.

That encounter stayed with us for a long time for when we returned home we seemed liked changed people. My father and I never spoke about it but we both caught each other looking for more information first at the local library and later on with the internet. We could tell when the other had been looking because they had a certain look in their eyes, or body expression, which can't be fully explained. (Those who have been there know what I'm talking about.)

My father and I, for many different reasons, never took any more trips after that and he died many years later. I was executor of his will and had the grim task of clearing up his estate. Looking over his stuff I found a large collection of reports, books and maps of the castle, forest, and the surrounding area. I had no idea that he had done so and was quite amazed that he had kept it such a secret over the years.

I suppose clearing out his place took me longer than necessary because I was fascinated by what he had. I kept all that I found because they were some of my strongest memory of my father and didn't want to get rid of them. I knew something had to be done with them but, at that time, wasn't sure what I was going to do with them and put them into storage and nearly promptly forgot about them as life overtook me.

Since the time I decided to write about this and started collecting and re-reading all the many dust filled articles, books, and other scraps of information that I had put into storage, many years ago, I have visited the castle ruins. It was early morning and that same odd, eerie feeling that I felt as a boy was still there. This time, thinking of my dad and I there together many years ago, I boldly managed to enter through the gate, and walk several steps, but couldn't go any further. But the green bush was still seen in the distance and was the only thing immediately recognizable.

In the distance laid the ruins of the great hall and other places which appeared too dangerous, for me, to try and explore as I was getting old and the exertion needed might have been too great for someone like me to undertake. Some have journeyed over there and have reported odd sights of which, again, they could never fully explain.

I did manage to bring my camera and took some photos. However, later upon viewing the photos there was nothing there.

The photos I took before and after the castle visit were fine; the photos of the actual castle visit turned out black. No one has been able to explain to me how this could happen because it was a nearly new camera.

I also journeyed to the forest during the same visit. It was indeed dense, and I barely managed to enter into it. One could see the outline of a trail, but it was difficult to continue walking without spending time removing the obstacles that were strewn on the tail. But as it was getting late, and the trees covered the remaining sunlight, I decided to leave and return the next day with proper equipment.

There is no car park near the ruins so one must park off the road which passes nearby. The local government of Fairwinds, after many complaints by tourists and even the locals, had built a rough car park that isn't paved nor regularly maintained. The car park is still an hour walk to the ruins so be prepared for a very long day especially if you wish to visit the forest as well.

When I woke up the next day, I was besieged by a number of minor incidents which one could chalk up to coincidences but ultimately delayed my quest, so I couldn't return to the forest because the next day I had to return home and family matters. I have yet to return there again and perhaps may never return.

Like most people I stayed at the coastal city of Fairwinds as well and explored their archives. Their archives doesn't contain much of those days I suppose because of the damage caused to the town during the various wars which raged in and around the region. There are a few historical references but you really have to spend time and dig deep into whatever they have. The archivists there are friendly but seem to try their hardest to dissuade you from delving deeper into their vaults. They rather talk about the success of their town rather than a heap of rubble that only a few tend to visit.

Like most tourists I also visited the tomb of the King Oliver and Queen Jessica of Fairwinds. While the tourist marker is in the local language I was able translate most of it (The city does not seem to be inclined to translate the marker into any other language.). The key line, for me, stated that King Oliver greatly expanded the territory and which was enhanced by a printed map that showed the Kingdom of Fairwinds expanding, to nearly the present day boundaries, during the reign of Oliver.

The following is a collection of historical fact, unclear statements of those who try to describe what they have seen, and just guessing to fill in large gaps of what has been recorded. The reader must decide how much is fact and how much is just conjecture.

Before I proceed any further, I must state that I firmly believe these ruins are indeed the legendary Castle Aldermount but I have no proof that would hold up in a court of my peers. Just a strong feeling and circumstantial anecdotes which could mean anything. Yet, facts and evidence remain that strongly suggest I, and others like me, are right.

PART ONE

This story, like any good story, started once upon a time there was a king and queen who lived in Castle Aldermount and were kind and generous to their kingdom. They were generous in their trade agreements and often the first to send aid to other kingdoms that suffered disaster. They were also the kingdom that sent a large number of troops should that need arise in defense of various treaties.

It has been said that, during one of the many wars of in the region, they one time stripped the castle of most of its defenders. Then they marched towards the battlefield and successfully turned the tide towards victory.

The legend of Castle Aldermount started centuries before where it is said that the founder of Aldermount was divinely inspired to seek out a new place. He spent many years trying to find a suitable place until coming to the area of the present-day ruins. Where the founder came from no one seems to know and there is no general consensus of this matter except, perhaps, that he probably came somewhere from the east. It's just taken as part of the story that is unknown and perhaps unknowable.

Over a long period of time the kingdom was continually known far and wide for its various successes. With the advent of the last King and Queen the successes continued but most writings were about their very beautiful daughter that they had. For it is the daughter for whom the story is about.

Legend has it that the name of the daughter was Princess Anne and she was an only child. It was soon after her birth that the local Bishop came to the royal chambers where the proud parents waited for a blessing on their daughter. They got something else. The Bishop saw the daughter and said, "This child shall be the rue of others and many mothers will weep because they cannot help.

"Beware of those who seduce with flowery language lest you are also seduced and follow them to the ruin of you and of generations yet unseen." At this he walked out leaving the parents wondering what had happened. There was never any blessing, then or later, and the word quickly made the rounds of the castle in hushed, fearful tones. The Bishop died a few months later.

She did grow up and was schooled in both matters of religion and of state. She showed a great knowledge of both and her peers and tutors were highly impressed. However, without the blessings of the Church, Anne was never able to formally participate in any religious service. She was only allowed to watch.

She would often ask why she wasn't allowed to formally participate in Church festivals. But her questions would meet with a soft smile and a nothing more. This, it is said, led her quest for greater knowledge that would eventually lead her to exploring ideas and later prove dangerous to everyone.

Before she started exploring new ideas a young Anne treated everyone with compassion (including all the animals) and they, in turn, treated her well. As she got older she would often be seen staying up late when one of the castle's animals were sick or she would lead the troops to find a peasant who was reported lost and long overdue to return to home or their work.

Anne grew to have a special interest in animals and could often be found in the stables when a mother animal was giving birth and she made sure the newborn animal had the greatest of care. Especially if the birth was difficult or if the newborn had other problems.

When an animal was sick Anne was again still seen in the stables seeing that everything possible was done for the wellbeing of the sick animal. It was said that her knowledge of animals rivaled the most learned animal doctors of not only her parent's kingdom but a few others that were close by and they had an alliance with like Fairwinds.

For lost children she took a special care in finding them. She would spend days and even weeks with the troops trying to find the lost child. It was very seldom that she could not for she seemed to have a talent in finding them.

For more happy occasions the child would often be seen riding on top of Anne's horse and Anne would be leading it by the reins. The troops would sound the horns and unfurl the royal flags announcing their triumphant return.

However, sometimes the discovery ended in tragedy. The troops formed a funeral procession and black banners were seen flying and no music was played as it entered the castle. Anne, and the Captain of the Calvary, would bring the child to the grieving parents and give them a small bag of coins to bury their child.

It was nearly universally agreed that Anne would grow up and become a great and respected ruler of the kingdom. But it wasn't meant to be as tragedy stuck during a most cold and bitter winter. It was during this time that both the king and queen were visiting the royal stables (they often made visits to various parts of the kingdom making sure everyone, including the animals, were safe and warm) when a horse panicked and started a stampede which kicked over a lit fire and the entire stable rapidly caught on fire and quickly burned to the ground. The king and queen tried to help calm the animals but alas, couldn't escape in time and perished in the flames.

The news quickly spread throughout the kingdom and the royal flags were taken down only to be replaced by the black banners of mourning. Only routine matters were conducted because no one was available, or wanted, to do anything more. For Anne hid in her room and was only briefly seen at official times before she disappeared again.

It was during this time, or perhaps even earlier, that rumors abound that she started to formally explore the Dark Arts in return to maintain her vain, radiant beauty all her life. Her quest to master the Dark Arts and maintain her beauty seems to be have become an overwhelming obsession at this stage in her tragic life.

Power and beauty seduced handmaidens could be see going in and out of Anne's room at all hours of day and night and strange lights were seen under her door at night while non-human muffled voices could be heard. Those, not privy to Anne's room shunned it and only those on official business dared to knock on the door. For Anne wanted to be left alone and, except for a chosen few, none dared to enter her room.

After the proscribed period of mourning came the coronation for Anne. She, and her handmaidens, exited her room full of indescribable beauty. They entered the throne room and the ceremony was performed and she was named Queen Anne of Aldermount and with all the titles and decrees that were associated with that. She received her crown and scepter and pledge to defend Aldermount from all enemies whoever they may be or whatever guise they may undertake.

She sat on the remaining throne (as the other one had been taken away) and the room hushed as everyone waited for her first words as Queen. She looked around the room and received a parchment from one of her handmaidens and started to proclaim; to those in the room it was reported that all were in shock at what was heard.

First, it was not enough to be loyal to Aldermount. Citizens of the kingdom had to be loyal to Anne alone and be ready to sacrifice their lives in unconditional obedience to an oath. Further, everyone must take it in front of the Queen, or her handmaidens, or be arrested and charged with disloyalty and treason to the state.

The proclaimed oath would be: "I swear I will be faithful and obedient to the leader of the Aldermount Kingdom and people, Queen Anne, to observe the law, to conscientiously fulfill my official duties and be prepared at all times to give my life to show my loyalty to this oath."

After the oath was stated then all the handmaidens stood in from of Anne and were the first to show their loyalty under the new oath.

Finally, Anne declared that no animal was to remain in the kingdom and any found were to be killed. The killing of the animals was to begin immediately and the famed cavalry were to be converted to foot soldiers. Those who harbored an animal were to be treated as an enemy of the state and taken to the dungeon for a period of time.

There was murmur and protests over this decree. The Captain of the Cavalry protested the loudest saying that the cavalry needed horses to patrol the region and that other animals were needed to help with farming and other work. The Captain also pointed out it was Anne who was known to be kind to animals and what would that do to her reputation. The protests stopped when the Queen instantly killed her, and her second-in-command, with magic and leaving nothing but two piles of blacken dust on the floor that intrepid visitors claim can still be seen to this day.

Then Anne stood up, sternly looked around, and asked if there was anyone else who wanted to protest. None dared to answer the challenge so everyone remained silent.

To show that she was serious a caged dog was brought in. Anne got up from her throne, went to the cage, opened it and played with it for a while. Then she pulled out a knife and killed the dog leaving all those who saw it in a state of shock. She then calmly walked out of the room with her handmaids as everyone there opened a wide path for them and perfunctorily bowed in terror when she passed by.

The first place of this gruesome killing task took place in the remaining royal stables under the watch of Anne's handmaidens. There, each cavalry trooper was commanded to kill his or her own mount. The tears that must have been shed by the troops as they watched their beloved mounts die by their own hand must have been unbearable to many. After each mount was killed one of the handmaidens came over and made sure it was actually dead.

The guards, once friendly to the people, were assigned this grisly task and a giant wailing and sadness could be heard from all corners of the kingdom. They moved from house to house always under the direction of those handmaidens.

When all was finished more searches took place for the next several months before the Queen was satisfied with the job. Afterwards, periodic searches were made and to the surprise of many more animals were found. Rewards were also posted to report neighbors who harbored any animal.

The people took no pleasure in it and often were seen with a tear in their eyes. It has been said that some let the animals escape and reported their lost. The Queen seemed to know what they did and those that let animals escape were not seen again.

Animals, that survived the initial onslaught, tried to flee the kingdom as best they could. They seemed to have heard it from various sources. Birds had the easiest time to flee but many of them were shot down by arrows of the guardsmen and the magic of the handmaidens. Land animals rushed the various gates (some were left open by the guards) and escaped. However, many of these animals were slain as they tried to escape.

In the center of the courtyard a large altar was erected and the dead animals were burned there day after day; night after night and it never stopped for months. The macabre ceremonies were conducted by the Queen's handmaidens that mocked the faith that the people had come to know and believed in.

Fire and smoke could be seen for miles around the kingdom and emissaries, from other kingdoms, were sent to see what the cause was. Upon their return to their own kingdom they sadly reported their findings (Even their horses were not spared from the Queen's rule and often an emissary could be found walking back to their own kingdom).

Within a short time, Queen Anne's kingdom stood alone without an ally in the world. For those kingdoms maintained a watchful eye on Anne's domain and made sure no one from there entered their own territory. Those that tried to escape from Aldermount were either turned back or slain if they resisted. No kingdom wanted anything to do with Aldermount. Animals, however, were the only exception and all were welcomed who were able to escape the terror.

The Queen's next major proclamation was the outlawing of the old faith. A new faith was to be instituted and anyone still practicing the old faith would be punished severely. The places of worship were desecrated and new icons were installed. The icons have been described as a mockery of the true faith. While some practices were kept most were discarded and people lost their faith. However, some were able to secretly maintain some of the practices of the old faith but they always greatly feared that neighbors, or even their own family members, would turn them in. All would be required to learn the new faith and follow its tenants to the letter and without questions.

With the loss of animals for farming people had to do harder labor. Crops yields went way down as the people couldn't farm big areas anymore. People barely were able to produce meager quantities that they were barely able to survive on.

Both the old and the young died of lack of food and water for even the clouds, it has been said, did not produce enough water for food nor for drinking. Those that died were buried in a common grave and to this day it has never been found. Perhaps the darkness of the castle swept them away to a so far away place that it yet to be discovered. Or perhaps, no one has ever looked in the right spot or dug deep enough.

The people lived miserably. Hope had mostly disappeared only to be replaced by fear. Those that dared to journey beyond the gate, and became lost, became fewer and fewer as the troops were forbidden to search for anyone (for they were delegated to provide security from all animals that dared to return). Those family members that did manage to go look for the lost often either never found them or found them dead. It was rare that anyone was found alive due to lack of food.

PART TWO

What happened to the animals? As previously mentioned many died and others, that did escape, found refuge in neighboring kingdoms. But a large majority of the escaped traveled hard and fast to the dense forest that's hours walk from Aldermount. There, they counted their living and they buried those that died because of the dangerous travel.

Upon entering the forest they tried to find family members or even just animals of the same type. Over the weeks the numbers added up; birds were the most numerous but small animals were also counted as well as fast horses. Even the occasional cow or pig wandered in and was made welcomed.

To the surprise of all the escaped animals they found, in the center of the forest the ruler of the forest- an old, wise owl living alone in an old tree overlooking a clearing. How long had the owl lived there? No one knows but, again rumors, suggest that he had been there for a very long time and seemed to know the plight of the animals. The owl gently greeted them all, seemed to know the right words to help those to forget what had happened to them and helped them to start a new life in their new home.

The owl took care of them and in time all the animals settled down into a new life. Each group of animals was given a place to live and duties to perform for the benefit of all. Guards were posted near the edge of the forest and often warned the others when the Queen's army approached. But nothing ever happened except for a few moments of excitement before the humans turned back the way they came. The owl never seemed surprised by them turning back.

Over the course of the seasons individual animals decided to go back to Aldermount and see what was going on mostly because they were curious. The owl never tried to dissuade them nor even council against this action. The owl just watched silently as various animals left on their own and watch them until they were out of sight before going back to whatever was important at the time. Most of the animals never came back. Those that did were often wounded and told of the sad plight of the people and the harrowing escape of themselves. Not many ventured to go back but there was always someone who got bored in the forest and wanted some adventure and didn't believe the stories told.

One by one they told their stories and one by one they were always the same. For the people they no longer farmed large tracts of land but instead most barely were able to scratch out a small plot to maintain their needs. The old and the young were even forced to work just to get enough food to get by. There seemed to be no hope but only fear as they looked around towards the hated guards and the handmaidens.

For the guards, and handmaidens, seemed to be everywhere. Often, when one wasn't looking or seemed to be distracted, they would just show up at different places and conduct a search. Sometimes nothing was found and a silent sense of relief was seen as the troops went away leaving a mess for the people to clean. Other times people would be hauled away and perhaps never to be seen again in which case surviving family member had more duties to perform. The guards also looked unhappy but seemed to also fear the handmaidens and the wrath of the queen if they failed to do their assigned duties.

The Queen was hardly seen but often spoken of only in hushed, feared tones. Her handmaidens, on the other hand, were always seen roaming around the castle walls making sure all decrees were being properly obeyed. They also conducted religious rituals on the altar and made periodic inspections of the houses and grounds. Nothing seemed to escape their notice and occasionally someone was being taken away by the guards with a handmaiden grinning nearby.

Escaping from the wraith of the Queen, for the animals, was also the same. They were often found out, chased and attacked. Sometimes the story would be of their companion who either gallantly covered an escape or just got unlucky.

For the survivors the terrors of the escape were told and how they were nearly found out and nearly killed. About how the guards, and handmaidens, chased after them for days and found nothing. How they found cover and barely even dared to breathe because they feared to be discovered. But luck, if you could call it that, was with them and they managed to make it back to the forest wounded but alive to recall their sad tales.

Over time the number of animals that tried to go back got fewer and fewer. But every so often someone tried and the results were the same. With less eyewitness reports the legends of Aldermount grew larger. So that one could never tell what was actually true and what was just legends and rumors.

Time and seasons passed until one day, in the spring, the owl called all the animals together. At the beginning the owl held many talks but over time these became fewer and fewer and the owl could be seen talking with small groups and individuals about different problems or ideas. Everyone was curious to know what was to be said.

At the appointed time the owl spoke from his tree. "My friends," he began, "I have spent some time among the people and I have great compassion for them. For they are without hope and faith. People live and die, and no one seems to care because they believe they live for nothing and there is nothing to live for. Many take their own lives in the belief that there is something better than the Queen."

How the owl spent time with the people is something no one knows. It is true the owl often went missing from the forest for a few days before his return. No one knew where he went and no one dared to ask. It was just a matter of faith that they accepted his words as true for what he said in the past was always true.

"We must give them hope," the owl continued. "For without hope they just live and suffer and see nothing of value." The owl stopped and looked around, "I have a plan that will instill great hope in them but someone needs to go to Aldermount to be a messenger of hope and faith. Who will go?"

The crowd was stunned and hushed. It was several moments before anyone spoke. "The queen is evil," some animal said. "You know the decrees she made about death to all animals that are found there." At the mention of the decrees many mothers gathered their young ones around them and held them close.

"If you have already been there," said another, "why don't you go back and do it yourself? We don't want to risk anything for such a foolish endeavor. You must think we are foolish to throw away our lives for a fool's game. We are safe and happy here." Many nodded and voiced their support for these kinds of statements.

After everyone became quiet again a small voice could be heard from the back, "Here I am; send me." Everyone looked around to find who spoke these words and all they could find was a gray, forlorn and pathetic bunny that was standing alone. One of his ears was bent downwards and his fur was dirty and sometimes missing.

Many smiled and let out a small laugh and demanded the bunny be silent. The bunny ignored everyone and repeated louder, "Here I am; send me!"

The owl called the bunny to the front and an opening was made by the animals. As the bunny approached the owl a few animals started to quietly whisper gossip, made other remarks about the bunny and everyone just stared.

The bunny stopped just below the branch where the owl was, looked up, and waited. Everyone was quiet. The owl fluttered down to ground and stood in front of the bunny. "Why do you want to go?" the owl asked.

"I am stupid. No one likes me and I have no friends. I am not as smart as some of the animals. I cannot climb trees or swim in the water or fly in the sky. I cannot do anything! No one will miss me if I something bad happens to me and I suppose many here would be happy if I did not come back."

The King of the Forest walked around the bunny and then stood in front of him and said, "You are very brave. More brave than all the animals that are here. Come with me for we have much to discuss for you will leave tonight because there is no moon and it will give you cover to go." With that the owl and the bunny walked away from the group leaving them in awe and puzzlement of what just happened.

Sometime later both the owl and the bunny stood at the edge of the forest. To all that were present the bunny was cleaned up. He didn't have any missing patches of fur and his bent ear stood upwards. The King of the Forest gave the bunny a weapon and some eggs then said, "Put these colored eggs in the center of town in the spot where I told you. When the people find them it will give them hope and make them happy. Your reward will be greater than you can imagine."

The bunny silently took the eggs and started hopping to the town on his dangerous mission. But he was extremely happy, for the first time in his life, because someone had called him brave and he wonder what his reward would be.

The King of the Forest had told the bunny what route to take and where to hide. How to hide from the Queen's patrols that roamed about seeking animals or invaders of any kind. It was hard but the bunny managed to get to the castle undetected.

The next few days the animals held a vigil waiting to see if the bunny returned or not. They waited for several days and no sign of the bunny. Rumors began to drift in saying the bunny had indeed succeeded on his mission but others denied it saying there was no proof. Then most of the animals were sad and they didn't even know his name.

Because the bunny accomplished his mission the King of the Forest (he seemed to know about the mission and everyone just accepted it as fact) ordered that once a year only a bunny would deliver colored eggs to the people of the town. This would give the people hope and happiness and to remember a very brave bunny who thought no one liked him.

In the forest, rumors abound, you can see a statue of the brave bunny if you know where to look.

What happened afterwards? The bunny did indeed make it to Aldermount and placed the eggs around the bush and the hated altar. The Queen was furious as she, and some of her escort, unexpectedly encountered the bunny as he tried to make his escape after completing his task.

The encounter between the bunny and the Queen is the stuff of legends and rumors. The Queen used her magic and the bunny had a sword that he used to dodge, parry and hop around her dark magic. In the end the Queen was a little faster but the bunny fought bravely to the end, with a glad heart, finally understanding of his reward.

In the morning, the people noticed colored eggs (but no sign of the struggle just hours before) hiding in and around the bush and altar that was located in the center of the courtyard. They gathered them up and searched for more. The Queen proclaimed that anyone found with an egg would be punished and launched a search of all the houses for any egg that the people might have found and kept.

Many eggs were found and the people were indeed punished. However, some eggs were never found and these were kept hidden where only a few knew about its existence because they feared their neighbors would report them. Sometimes not even those living in the house knew of the existence of the eggs.

If one stood in the midst of where eggs were hidden people found a sense of calm and peace. Many found that any family troubles were soon settled, and work became easier and lighter for them. Even watchful neighbors, who came to visit, seemed to overlook odd behaviors of the host family.

The guards, and the dreaded handmaidens, who came to search seemed not to be affected by the eggs. The guards feared the handmaidens and the handmaidens seemed immune to the effect of the eggs. The searches were ruthless and when eggs were found they were taken to the altar and smashed while the family was taken to the dungeons for countless interrogations.

However, in the following years more eggs appeared. Even the Queen could not stop it though she posted guards since the events seem to happen around the same time each year. Also, during that time period people would stroll over to the bush and innocently look and see if eggs were hidden. If so, they would try to distract the guards (for there were many of them) and try to grab an egg or two. Some made it but many did not and were dealt with according to the wishes of the Queen.

Over the course of years several things happened. First, the guards of Aldermount tried to expand the territory by going forth and killing all animals that were near the borders with them. Some of the guards that entered into the Aldermount forest never came back.

PART THREE

Another thing that happened was that the King of Fairwinds strengthened his borders with troops but short, brief encounters between opposing troops were bound to happen and not in a good way. The Fairwinds troops stood little chance against the handmaidens who just seemed to laugh at the Fairwinds, and other castles, troops. The commanding officer, of the defeated troops, made their reports back to the various castles and these reports were sent to all the other castles in the area.

The only way to end these deadly skirmishes, according to the various rulers surrounding Aldermount, was to go to war against them. Thus, a council of war was called and plans were drawn up to finish the horrors of their neighbor once and for all. Everyone knew casualties would be high but agreed it would be worth the ending. King Oliver of Fairwinds was put in overall command as he, not only lived the closest, but would put up the most troops for the final march against dreaded Queen Anne and her handmaidens.

Perhaps the story should continue in the words of the King Oliver:

Forces from all over the land, far and near, were encamped near the territory of Aldermount preparing for the final push onto that dire land. The Council of War was in session making final preparations that would occur in the early morning when the Captain of the Watch ran into the tent and told us to come outside and see what is happening. Not knowing what to expect we gathered up our weapons and went outside.

We didn't have to ask the good Captain what was the problem was for we all instantly saw it ourselves. It appeared to be a large, fiery figure rising up to the heavens from the direction of Aldermount. It moved in the direction towards us but never threatened our position before moving upwards and out of sight.

Later, we all agreed that traveling with this demonic figure were several smaller black figures. One appeared to be wearing a crown. A few claimed they saw the look of horror on the faces of the black figures but no one could agree on that. But the one figure wearing a crown most of us agreed upon.

No one knew what the meaning of this sorcery was but we suspected it could anticipate nothing good. We, therefore, ordered the Captain of the Guard to send messengers to our outposts to double the guards and maintain a constant vigil. Without even writing this as a formal order we knew it would be done because in a few hours, just before sun breaks, we would advance and not many would sleep tonight after what they just saw.

I stepped into my tent and changed clothes into something less kingly because I wanted to see firsthand how the moral of the troops were. I put on an officer's cloak and wandered about the

32

forward areas. Most troops seemed to understand the business at hand and, those that weren't on guard duty, spent time cleaning their armor or sharpening their weapons. A few were seen trying to sleep but it seemed to be in vain for most of them gave up and just sat quietly staring into the darkness.

I went over to another armies' position making sure I had my pass signed by me so I could pass over to other kingdom's area of responsibility. They too were getting ready for battle and the preparations for them were about the same as for us.

I noticed a group of young soldiers being talked to by whom it appeared to be a senior officer. I moved closer and listen to what they were being told. This senior officer had the look of experiencing many hard campaigns said: "Look around you and you will see your brothers, sisters and fathers standing next to you. We will go into battle soon and you may not see some of them again. Come to terms with that right now. They may be lying on the ground with their guts hanging out from a deadly blow. This is war and she is a cruel mistress and does not take pity; nor does she choose sides of the armies. But for those that survive they will know the sweetest feeling that they have endured the greatest hardships that will come with the morning.

"We do not march for honor or glory. Therefore, there will be no awards given in this campaign. For the Count doesn't want *heroes and the dead don't need them. We march and die simply because it is our duty. Living and surviving are its own rewards.*

"Remember to obey your commanders, be watchful of your surroundings and trust the faith. Now get ready for battle."

The soldiers quietly dispersed and I was going to talk with that senior officer but she had disappeared among the crowd of recruits. It was a pity for I wanted to know her name just in case she was among the fallen.

I walked over to another army and observed their actions. Many of the soldiers were, like most others, sitting and waiting. However, a large group of them attended a religious service. The respect and reverence shown was greatly admired by me. I stayed until the end of service and everyone just got up and walked back to their units. There was no talking but just a holy silence that you could almost feel.

It was getting close to the time and I walked back to my tent and changed into my proper armor and got weapons ready.

When I exited my tent it was time to go. Messengers were running back and forth with last minute instructions but nothing would stop this final assault. I had nothing to add so I said nothing but went to the forward command post and waited for the battle to begin and soon heard the horns of command sounding; it was starting.

Upon arriving at the command post reports were already coming in stating that our troops had engaged in combat with Aldermount but the defenders didn't put up much of a fight and were surrendering in large numbers. I quickly put more troops into battle and urged everyone to go forth with great haste. I sent messages to the commanders of the front that they still need to be prepared for Aldermount's handmaidens to make their appearance and thus slow down our advance. The appearance of the handmaidens never happened.

More reports came that troops were just giving up without a fight. We disarmed them and then moved them to our rear for further questioning. What they said didn't make much sense but we figured they would fight at the castle for surely the Queen would be there and make her last stand.

I rode forward as fast as I could just to make sure the reports were true. Not only were the soldiers giving up but we encountered many townsfolk fleeing from the castle with what could only be described as one of shock and relief. We also sent them to our rear and pushed forward to what should be the final battle.

When we finally got to the castle what should have been a solid structure ready to defend itself was a total ruin. Not much was left of it and it was hard to recognize any place that I had visited in my youth.

Before entering the castle grounds I sent messengers back to our lines having them report Aldermount is ours and to treat all those who surrender with compassion and respect. To those that resisted our troops know their duties. I also asked that the timetable be moved up and that reinforcements be sent to the area to make sure the castle, and the surrounding areas, are truly ours.

I entered the castle grounds with the first of our troops and ordered them to search for any survivors and, above all, to find the Queen.

After giving the commands I, and my staff, went over to where the banner of Aldermount flew and took it down. We raised up the banner of Fairwinds, claimed it as part of our territory, and said a small prayer of thanks for the success of this campaign.

The senior officer of the first troops made his report. They had found a few survivors and are now starting to dig them out of the rubble. There was no sign of the Queen or her court and every building was now nearly a pile of stones. Not even the plants, except for the bush that my command post was set next to, was growing; all seemed to have died.

The altar that was next to my tent was, on the warning of the High Priest, torn down. It was rebuilt as a true altar to the true faith and he sanctified it. By the end of the day we had held our first religious service there and all those that didn't have duties attended it.

Reports from the survivors told a terrifying tale for their stories seemed to be all the same. They said that many were sleeping when a horrible noise sounded and all the buildings started to shake and crumble. The lucky ones ran out as fast as they could, with few or no possessions, and looking towards the castle hall they saw a large, fiery figure raise up to the skies with several smaller, black figures surrounding it. The figures all screamed a defying scream with caused some people to go mad and the rest just turned around and ran as fast as they could to escape the ongoing destruction.

Upon learning what the survivors were telling us I gave the order that they could return and try to salvage what they could from where they once lived. However, it was to be done under the watchful eyes of our troops as we didn't know what to expect from them. They seemed to expect this as they say they have been under watching eyes for years. With this some of our troops helped them as best they could while other troops continued their vigil.

Nothing happened and most were orderly and we treated them with kindness and helped them in their needs when we could. After they had picked up their belongings we sent them to the rear where they could rest and try to recover and decide what to do with their lives. All decided to leave their previous life in Aldermount and seek a new life someplace else. We will divide them up among the kingdoms that joined in this campaign.

Families will be able to stay together and the rest will be decided by lot of where to go.

We asked how they ate without meat for all those years. Many were embarrassed to answer. The answers we did get consisted of them living off of vegetables and occasionally smuggled in some rare meat which tended to be eaten in secret and in the dark.

We stayed in the area for several days continuing looking for the Queen and helping and finding more survivors. I studied the building where the great hall once was. I was shown by my aide, who was present at the Queen's coronation, two black marks where the Captain and her second-in-command were killed. My aide mentioned that the marks were just as black today as they were years ago. But the body of the Queen was never found. We buried the dead and mourned the losses.

The highest official we have so far captured and identified was the Chancellor. When questioned about the Queen all he would do was sob and then scream: "She is going to kill me!" We later found him dead of self-inflicted wounds with a ghastly look on his face that few would ever forget. The campaign was over, it was time to return home.

Upon leaving the castle the High Priest said to me: "The castle is yours but leave it be. Do not occupy it, nor rebuild it for it will all be in vain."[1]

I looked at him and he seemed to know what I wanted from him. "Leave it as a remembrance of the past and as a warning to the future." With that he left my side and walked with the troops. It had started to rain so I just pulled my cloak more closely around me.

King Oliver later wrote:

I have finally finished reading the reports of the Aldermount campaign. One of the more interesting things is that troops from another kingdom advanced on the forest beyond the castle. I was happy to read it was the senior officer, of whom I heard giving a speech to her troops prior to the battle, that commanded the advance to the forest which was in their area of responsibility.

The officer reported that upon nearing the forest the entire command stopped because it seemed to be a holy and sacred place and none dared to enter. The officer respected the decision and commanded that no one was to enter the forest while waiting

---

[1] It has been reported that over the decades developers have tried to do something with the area. But numerous reports have shown that when development was attempted workers, and managers, either got sick or died and equipment failed to operate.

further orders. Troops were posted to search for survivors and any
soldier that wanted to continue that futile struggle.

Armies, coming from the opposite side of the forest
reported the same thing. No one dared to enter. A small shrine was
hastily erected to give thanks for such a miracle for what was
expected to be a grisly campaign.

Perhaps I will visit the Aldermount forest after these
negotiations are finished. There is something about battle that is
far more exciting than these current negotiations no matter how
necessary they are.

Comparing the two I remember the words of my old
mentor: "Negotiations may cost far less than war, or infinitely
more: for war cannot cost more than one's life." Still rings true
today.

The troops that are stationed there report that no animals
can be found. Animal noises can be heard from the Aldermount
forest but orders have been given not to enter it. I wonder why
even when we put animals in the area they seem agitated and wish
to leave. My own horse, when I was there was the same way. I
suppose it only stayed with me because it was trained to do so.
After we left the area it seemed to calm down greatly.

I stumbled upon the following part almost by accident and
nearly discarded it as seemingly unimportant. It was in the King's
diary and written many years after the Aldermount campaign and it

appears to be in his old age; perhaps a few years before his death as there is no date on it.

My friend, the High Priest, died last night and I am deeply sadden. It wasn't unexpected as he was ill for a long time but never seemed to complain and continued to listen to those who came to his bedside. His last words were, "I have done my duty to my faith and I hope it is enough for my judgment to come." With that he passed away with a smile of content and we, who were there, wept bitterly and unashamed.

He was not only the spiritual advisor to Fairwinds but I considered him to be a good friend and a wise sage. He often accompanied us on many military campaigns and was there during the Aldermount saga.

I have many fond memories of him but perhaps the most strongest was the time he came into the library when I was there at night and alone. I didn't hear him come in for he often came in quietly and unannounced. I was intent on my work when something caused me to look up and was startled to see him standing in front of me. "Writing the Aldermount story?" he inquired.

I don't know how he knew for I never mentioned it to him. It was my custom not to withhold information he sought from me and I saw no reason to start now. "Yes," I said. "Is there anything I can do for you?"

He came closer to my table, glanced over my papers, and said, "The glory of a good man is the testimony of a good conscience. Therefore, keep your conscience good and you will always enjoy happiness, for a good conscience can bear a great deal and can bring joy even in the midst of adversity.

"But an evil conscience is ever restive and fearful. Sweet shall be your rest if your heart does not reproach you. Do not rejoice unless you have done well. Sinners never experience true interior joy or peace for there is no peace for the wicked. Even if they say: 'We are at peace, no evil shall befall us and no one dares to hurt us,' do not believe them; for the wrath of truth will arise in due time, and their deeds will be brought to naught and their reign will perish.

"Perhaps no one will read your accounts. For who can truly say what the future will hold for us after we are gone. Look at what happened to Anne for many may remember her and her unnerving deeds. But what about the bunny?

"Remember that shadows and spirits are often employed by demonic overlords to act as emissaries to us mortals. The Lord of the Dark Arts has employed many such creatures to try and corrupt us. Sad to say that most times they are successful and those are the most remembered.

"Yet others are called and served with greatness and no one will ever notice them either now or later.

"When words laced with honey are accompanied by the smell of sulfur, it is best to turn away with great haste, lest you fall prey to their infernal preaching."

With that he turned around and walked away leaving me wondering what he meant. Over the years I have asked again and again what he meant by those words. All he would say was "Reflect more," with a smile before turning away.

I have done my best to stamp out what is evil and to try and instill good where I can. I have used military, economic and diplomatic means to help with other kingdoms so they can also do so. But, to this date I still have no idea what he knew nor what he wanted to tell me. Now, I shall never know for sure.

I just hope and pray that whoever is selected as High Priest is just as kind, loyal and reverent as he was. Especially now that my beloved wife has been laid to rest many years ago. I need someone I can turn to in my age.

Looking at other records it does indeed to appear (but not definite) to have been written a few years before his death. His wife and friend were gone before him and he had time to finish his Aldermount saga.

The Aldermount saga has been around for a long time and can be found in many bookstores and online. However, they have been heavily edited and re-edited so many times it's hard to know what was original and what has been added or subtracted from it.

EPILOGUE

Since I started writing this I have had a strong urge to return to Aldermount one last time. Thus, one day, I boldly walked onto the grounds and saw the bush which was still green and still growing. I stood next to it and thought of King Oliver standing near me giving commands, raising the Fairwinds banner over the castle walls, and building a shrine near the spot and giving thanks for such an unexpected victory.

It is easy to see where the great hall once stood and image the horrors of that night when the entire foundation shook and a fiery figure raised up from the hall. One could almost hear the screams of whoever was taken up by that figure.

You could also image the people fleeing from their collapsing homes with nothing more than what they wore. I suppose some families waited too long for their loved ones and didn't escape. They are, like all those that died that night, buried in a common grave that was hastily built by the Fairwinds alliance.

The cemetery is just outside the walls of Aldermount but it is mostly overgrown because no one seems to want the job to maintain it. Yet visitors seem to do the job because they are, like everyone else who visits, looking for something. People leave small tokens to mark that they have been here and respect all those that died on that terrible night.

While standing there I felt a sense of relaxation but also felt something watching over me and giving me a warning of not to touch the bush. The sense was not one of anger but hard to put into words. I looked around the bush and didn't see anything unusual but still I dared not touch it.

It then started to rain and I took out and unfurled my umbrella. I then walked out of the courtyard leaving behind the grounds that were quickly becoming rain soaked. At the old gate entrance I turned around for one last looking. Peering towards the bush and, for a moment, thought I saw a bunny peaking its face out and looking directly at me. Before I could do anything it was gone and to this day I don't know if what I saw was real or just a play on my imagination (especially since the distance and the rain were great). I suppose it doesn't really matter. I have no plans on returning there in my retired age and what I believe is good enough for me.

HISTORY OF A TOWN

PROLOUGE

If you are one of the many thousands of people who have driven US Highway Route 101 along the Pacific Ocean I suppose you stopped at some town, got some gas and even perhaps a bite to eat before going on with your journey. As you quickly drove in and out of that faceless, non-descript town you never gave any thought about that town except as a place to fulfill your needs.

Near the southern border of the state of Oregon there is one town that you may have stopped at. This town is called St. Tremblay which currently has a population of just under 2000 people. It was once a thriving coastal town over its history but with the advent of Interstate 5 it has slowly dwindled to its current population. I spend my childhood growing up there.

My father died there and he is buried in the local cemetery. His home (and the home I grew up in) was on the outskirts of town and when I came back and went through his stuff I couldn't stay at his home for there was too many memories. So I stayed at one of the tourist hotels near the water.

I eventually was able to sell his house, with many tears, because I have lived my life someplace else. Maybe I could have kept it, retired to it but my life has moved on from a small town where everyone knows your name to where I write this.

The schools that I grew up in are now all gone. They have combined into one school for all the grades. I suppose that one day they will even close that school down and will bus the students to a school in the next town.

Beyond the gas stations and restaurant, that you see at the US 101 exit, there is not much left of its history. There is a runway that is being taken care of by the county and was once used by the military. There are some hangers there to house private aircraft.

You can also see the remains of a control tower that once dealt with weekly commuter shuttles to Portland when I was growing up. It was these commuter trips that started my summer holidays with my dad and the journeys around the world.

Now, the runway and hangers are being used by local private pilots for keeping up pilot's license up to date as well as a base for local search and rescue missions that occur more frequently than one would like to imagine.

On the coast there is a nearly shipping terminal that once housed a naval anti-submarine squadron but now houses some fishing and tourist boats. Parking is usually easy to find and you can walk to the boats and get one of the captains to take you on a trip either to try your hand at ocean fishing or to watch whales that migrate up and down the coast.

What you are about to read is a brief history of the town. I have spent many hours in both the states of Oregon and

Washington archives as well as the National Archives researching and asking lots of questions. I have also written letters, and again, spent time, and travel, in both the UK and French archives.

Non-English names and spellings have often been changed to their English, and modern, equivalence so the reader doesn't have to continually try to translate words they may not understand.

PART 1

The city of St. Tremblay, Oregon is named after the French naval captain Guy St. duTremblay who was born May 18, 1754 in the town of Trouville-sur-mer. He was one of the two surviving children of the family and was baptized and confirmed in Our Lady Star of the Sea Catholic Church.

That church is no longer in existence as it was heavily destroyed by Allied bombings during World War 2. These bombings were in support of the future Allied landings in Normandy as well as trying to destroy the German E-boats that were based there. The town was also subjected to British commando raids early in the war because of the presence of a radar station that helped Kriegsmarine E-boats attack Allied shipping in the English Channel.

After the war it was decided not to rebuild the church and to move the surviving relics to the other churches (which apparently included the baptismal font that St. duTremblay was baptized in. Also, written church records were part of the items moved).

Growing up he was educated at one of the Christian Brothers schools and spent time, during holidays, helping his father with tend the fishing boat his family owned. He loved the sea as much as he loved his family and his faith.

On his 14th birthday he asked his parents blessing for the next stage in his life. The blessing was given and both he and his father set sail to the port of Le Havre. Upon arrival he joined the navy as an officer candidate.

By the time he was 21 he had sailed around the world and visited almost all the colonies that France possessed at that time. He learned everything about sailing ships and how to command them. He excelled at gunnery and was often posted as a gunnery officer on whatever ship he was serving on.

In 1776 his ship was docked at what is now New Orleans when he heard about the American colonies declaring their independence. He knew enough English to talk with the various American and English ships that ported there and found out their views on this news.

In his journal he wrote that he hoped the colonists would be successful in their endeavor but didn't know how they could do it without help from other countries to challenge British rule.

The answer to his question became clearer when his ship was ordered to Spanish Florida, in 1777, and assist the Spanish in supplying weapons and training for the Americans living near that border. His ship had to do supply runs from French held colonies, in the Caribbean, to Florida. It is clear he didn't like this duty, but he nevertheless did what duty was required of him.

Late in the following year he was promoted and made chief navigator of the frigate *Cardinal de Richelieu.* This was when France official joined the American Revolution. His ship was assigned to attack British ships as well as dealing with pirates that often plagued the Caribbean Sea.

There were no major actions against British shipping that the *Richelieu* engaged in. However, in mid-1779 there was a major hurricane that came through the Caribbean and nearly wrecked the ship. The ship was put into port at Haiti and repairs keep the *Richelieu* out of action until the middle of the following year.

In 1781, now promoted to second-in-command of the *Richelieu* they were ordered to join the French fleet, at Haiti, that was heading to the Americas to engage the British. They arrived prior to the fleet leaving the West Indies and were able to participate in both the Battle of the Chesapeake (damaging the British frigate *HMS Winter* in a close action duel) as well as the Battle of Yorktown.

After Britain formally surrendered to the Americans, St. duTremblay and the *Richelieu* were ordered to return home for some much-needed rest and repairs. There, he was able to successful pursue a relationship and marriage to Marie de la Foch. They had two children, but none appears to have survived into adulthood.

In 1785 St. duTremblay set sail again. This time he was promoted to captain of his own ship: the frigate *Norte Dame.* His orders were, once again, to proceed to an old familiar place- Haiti. Since it was also a new crew, he was instructed to train them in the duties of seamanship and the traditions of the navy by the time he arrived to his duty station.

On another tour of the Caribbean he was there when the Haitian Revolution began in 1791. His job was not only to suppress revolutionaries' coastal forts but also to intercept any goods that were supplied to the revolution by sea.

In mid-1792 he nearly lost his life and ship when it was caught unexpectedly by a hurricane that came through the area. He managed to get his ship back to port heavily damaged. He then returned to France just in time to see the beginnings of the Revolution there.

Near the end of the year, and on warnings of his friends that crowds were attacking those who appeared loyal to the king and Catholic Church, he and his wife were able to flee France before the mobs attacked their place. The commander of the ship had no love for the Revolution but also no love for the king or church. Their last sight of France was the burning of their house as crowds expressed their frustration of not being able to capture them.

They set sail for New Orleans to start a new life and away from all the revolutions that were consuming France. When they arrived, they learned about the execution of the king and the formation of a new government.

One of the first things they had to do was secure lodging and a job. With the money they have brought over they were able to accomplish the first task. After that was done, they appeared to have accomplished the second task by having St. duTremblay buying a fishing boat and hiring a crew.

The fishing boat appears to have been successful as they were able to buy a house near the docks. Here, Madam de la Foch was able to entertain various social elements of the city as well as her husband's crew and their wives.

They were active members of the famous St. Louis Cathedral and helped those in need when called upon by either the parish priest or the bishop.

While things seemed to go well for them tragedy struck hard. Madam de la Foch died, in April 1802 due to tuberculous and is buried in St. Louis Cemetery. It appears to have deeply affected St. duTremblay as he sold his boat and house and lived in a poor house near the church.

After mass on Christmas Day, 1803 he placed all his possession in a trunk, boarded a ship, and headed back to France. He knew there was still a price on his head for being an officer in the King's navy but he wanted to die on French, rather than American, soil.

PART 2

The ship docked in Le Havre and he was met by members
of the garrison. He was arrested and charged with being loyal to
the King and against the new republican government. He was lead
to prison to await his trial and execution. He calmly went while
many surrounding him mocked and spat on him. It was late at
night when he arrived at the prison.

He was thrown in with the rest of political prisoners
awaiting trail and probable execution. They didn't have long to
wait for the next morning they were all lead to a committee who
were to dispense justice in name of the Republic. They were all
found guilty of various crimes and sentenced to death as soon as
possible.

They were all then lead by to the prison to wait their turn
for the executioner. While some talked bravely of being loyal to
France others wept and said nothing but contemplated their own
existence that was soon to expire. St. duTremblay just prayed for
himself and those who he was with. Some mocked him while
others joined him knowing that they would have to face God and
His judgment soon.

The next day the guards came and the first to be removed
where those that mocked St. duTremblay and the others. Those that
joined him in prayer where the last ones to be lead away leaving

him alone in the cell to pray for those that once prayed with him as well as himself. That was all he could do while waiting for his turn.

He was in his cell alone for a few days and wondered if anyone remembered him. It was at this time that two people arrived, dressed in Republican uniforms, and asked for him specifically. He was surprised to see Republican officers asking for him.

They told him that he could either follow them and have a chance to serve Republican France or he could stay there and wait for his turn for death which wouldn't be long in coming. He choose to follow them and see where God was leading him.

They exited onto the street during the day. He hadn't seen sunlight for nearly two weeks and it was hard for him to keep up with his unnamed companions. But he did hear murmurs of the crowd and loud voices all talking about him. He ignored them all but did the best to keep up and say some prayers for his short-term deliverance.

When they finally arrived at a building he didn't recognize his eyes had finally adjusted to the sunlight. The guards of the building let them pass and he was lead up a couple of floors to a pair of large doors where more guards stood. The guards opened the door and the trio walked in.

It appeared to be a military headquarters and in the middle of the room was a large table surrounded by several military looking officers. When the doors opened they saw who was coming in and looked curiously upon the visitors.

One of the people, who was shorter than the others, in the room said, "You are Guy St. duTremblay?" It was answered with a nod. "I am Napoleon Bonaparte and I have need of your services.

"We are at war with the British, and others, and our naval forces are not doing well. We want to strike against the British where they don't expect it." Nothing was said.

"It has been said that you were one of the best gunnery officers in the former regime. With the Republic now gone, and their ways of abolishing the old military system it's hard to find anyone with your experience.

"I offer you a commute of your sentence and command of your own ship if you accept."

"What must I do?" St. duTremblay replied for the first time.

"Come here and look at this map." He did and saw it was a map of the New World. "You know I have sold Louisiana to the Americans because I didn't want it to fall into the hands of the British.

"But they still have Oregon area and all of Old France[2]. There they use it to trap animals for fur as well as whales for oil. I want to put a stop to it."

"I'm listening."

Napoleon spoke more. "There is a frigate in Bayonne that I offer you to command. Your orders are to sail to the Oregon waters, establish a base and attack the British merchant fleet that plies the waters around there.

"In exchange I will commute your sentence restore your name to the Empire of France."

Some days later St. duTremblay was in Bayonne at the naval docks. He knew about the British ships that patrolled offshore but that didn't greatly worry him. What really troubled him was that he knew British spies were around and he couldn't trust anyone. Therefore, he kept the mission to himself not letting anyone know lest they fall into British hands.

There was indeed a frigate for him to command but the crew needed lots of work. The second-in-command was a former Catholic who gave up his faith for the Republic. His name was Charles Borde and he hated Catholics and all that his former life stood for; he especially hated St. duTremblay for reminding him of his past.

---

[2] Modern day Canada

St. duTremblay worked on getting to know the crew. He watched them and often showed them how to do something when they couldn't do it. He made it look easy, especially at his age, and the crew respected him for it.

One day he saw one of his senior men striking a crewmember. He said nothing but later called a meeting of all his senior staff. "I saw one of you," he started, "striking a crewmember because he did something wrong. They are men and not cattle that you can strike at your own pleasure.

"We are going on a mission soon and we need to rely upon these men to do their jobs when the time comes. I want them to do it willingly and not out of fear.

"You are to train them as I have shown you. Explain to them what they don't know and show them what they don't understand.

"If I see any of you strike another man, on this ship, I will assign you to do that man's job. If there is any punishment to be given out it will be done by me alone.

"If any of you disagree with these rules then you are free to transfer off this ship before we sail.

"I also have a letter from the Emperor which states," he took out a paper from his tunic:

"Captain Guy St. duTremblay is acting under my direct orders in a matter of importance to all of France. All citizens of the Empire of France will aid him, without distinction of rank or station, as he sees fit.
Napoleon Bonaparte.

"I will write these up in the ship's log and they will be standard orders on this ship as long as I am in command. That is all."

It was near the end of the year that conditions were considered right to leave. The crew were trained, and it was a moonless night. The name of the ship was changed to something more proper: *Our Lady Star of the Sea.* St. duTremblay stood on the docks wearing a uniform of a commanding officer in the King's navy. Where he got it no one knew or dared to ask.

Soon a messenger arrived and was ushered to St. duTremblay. The messenger handed him the dispatch and went on his way wondering what he just saw. St. duTremblay paid no attention to the messenger's query but opened the letter and read it with interest. He then put the letter in his pocket and walked up the gangplank to his ship.

"Remove the gangplank and cast off all mooring lines," he commanded as he took his place near the wheel. The orders were carried out and the ship began to leave the dock and travel into the unknown.

The ship sailed into the Bay of Biscay and the only one talking was the captain and in a quiet voice. Guns were manned and ready for use if it came to that; everyone held their breath not knowing what to expect. However, no British ship appeared and the *Our Lady Star of the Sea* managed to sail into the dark night of the Atlantic and on a course known only to its commander.

St duTremblay wrote: *We have set sail and it feels good to have the wind at my back and the sea below me. For the next several months I need to train the crew and make sure we manage to complete our duty.*

I doubt that even if we are successful in our mission it will radically change the course of the conflict. But the only alternative, for me, is either death or prison. I'd rather sail under a sentence of death than live in prison as an exile.

The next day he called the crew together and said, "The first part of this journey is to Haiti where we will take on supplies for the rest of the mission.

"I will tell you where we are heading once we leave Haiti. Spies are everywhere," he looked at Charles Borde, "and we cannot take the risk of enemies of the state finding out what our mission is. That is all for now.

"Mister Borde, follow me to my cabin. "

Borde followed St. duTremblay to his cabin and the door was closed behind them. "I know you are writing reports about me," St. duTremblay started. "You are free to write and report them to whoever is interested in them.

"However, I will not stop this ship nor give you any support in delivering those reports. The only way you can deliver them is by swimming back to France. That is your choice.

"Also, do not attempt to stage a mutiny onboard and take over this ship. You will fail. Your only job is to be the first officer of this ship. Anything else will be met with punishment from me. Is that understood?"

Borde looked surprised that the captain knew about the reports. He looked down and said, "Yes, sir." Then he left the cabin.

It took a few weeks to sail to Haiti. During the course of the voyage the ship steered a course around other ships seen. They didn't want to be noticed by anyone and it was known that sometimes British commanders would fly a flag of France, or a neutral country, hoping to lure French ships close to them before they raised their true colors and engaged them in a ship to ship duel in which the French ships often lost.

When they arrived near Haiti they found that the land didn't belong to France anymore. Before they anchored there was a dispute with the Haitian government about if they could dock or not. It was decided that they could anchor but no one was allowed to leave the ship except for official duties. They stayed long enough to resupply the ship and set sail for its final destination.

St. duTremblay wrote: *In happier days I was here. In my lifetime I have seen the fall of the French empire. From when I was a boy with the surrender of New France, the selling of Louisiana and now this place. The France that I knew is no longer here. It is only a shell of its former self.*

But perhaps more important France has lost its faith. With the death of the King the faith has gone away and anyone who dares to practice it are arrested and killed.

Perhaps I might have been better if I stayed in Louisiana after the sellout, but my home is France and I always will belong to France no matter where the road may lead.

A few days more at sea St. duTremblay assembled the crew and spoke to them. "We are heading for the Pacific to wage war on the British. We will resupply again in Spanish territory of the Americas and then head northward to establish a base and attack British whaling ships in the area."

Surviving the passage through the Strait of Magellan they head northwards to Spanish lands in the Americas. They arrived at Monterey and after presenting his documents to Governor José Joaquín de Arrillaga who was surprised to see him.

"You have arrived? How was your journey?" Arrigllaga asked.

"My journey, so far, has been fair. Here are my documents and I wish my ship to be resupplied with the list presented and my men time to relax before doing their duty. It has been a long time since most have seen land."

"I understand. We will resupply your ship with food and other stuffs. As for your men they are free to enjoy what we have to offer but warn them that we will not tolerate any disorder.

"We also have some reports of what is north of us. Let us assemble in one hour and we will show you what we have."

"You should have no problem with my crew. Good day, sir!" With that St. duTremblay left and looked for the nearest church to offer his prayers of thanks for getting him this far and his crew safe.

It is recorded that his ship left Monterey on 15 July 1805 with maps and other document that the Spanish supplied showing various bays that were large enough to hold a frigate and also had enough material to start building a small post.

St. duTremblay wrote: *The service from the Spanish was fair and my ship is again ready to sail north. I have discussed my mission with the Spanish and they have shown me some maps of where their scouts have been north of Alta California. I have selected two possible locations where we can set up a small base and will check each one out when we arrive.*

The men were kept busy trying to get the ship ready as soon as possible. The language barrier was often a problem but many of the Spanish spoke some French and some of my officers spoke some Spanish. My men behaved properly and those that didn't were punished.

When duties didn't call me I was at church. It was sad for I was the only member of my ship to attend Mass and those that joined me were mostly the old; not many Spanish officials attended church and yet they all claimed to be Catholic; I wonder.

Now that we have set sail again, I look back on my life and find the only thing I have left are my faith, my duty, and the sea. Perhaps they are enough.

Several days later he wrote: *We have surveyed the bays the Spanish told us about. The first one seemed to be better suited for us and we will anchor there and scout the immediate area and see if there are anything that is hostile to us. Also, what food can be found there?*

By mid-August the camp seems to have been built: *The camp isn't like home but it does have the advantage of being on land. Tomorrow I shall take the ship out and carry out our orders.*

Reports from California have all suggested that British fishing ships continue to sail up and down the coast and should be easy to find. I hope so.

Ship logs report that several British merchant ships were destroyed by the end of August. But reports from the British commander in Vancouver's Island states that they are aware of merchant ships being attacked and that naval patrols were being increased in the area. It was stated that they thought the attacking ship were American because of the conflict with the Oregon country.

On September 12, 1805 the frigate *Notre Dame étoile de la mer* sailed out of her protected cove and went to seek out more ships to destroy. What it found was a pair of British frigates[3] with decks cleared for action and waiting. The British opened fired at long range and Marines were up on the sails waiting for the ships to get closer so they could shoot at their targets.

The battle didn't last long as the French were out gunned and the wind wasn't in their favor. The tide of the battle turned, for the British, when Captain Guy St. duTremblay was killed by a British Marine while ordering maneuvers that he hoped would achieve an escape.

Those who saw the death were stunned and Lieutenant Charles Brode assumed command. He knew he couldn't out duel

---

[3] These were the *HMS Oaksprite* which was lost in a Pacific storm in 1807 and the *HMS Princess Rachel* which was damaged by the *USS Guilford Courthouse* in 1813.

the ships so he did what he thought best – he surrendered by striking his colors.

The surrender was orderly and proper. Brode did ask for one thing and it was granted. He asked that Captain St. duTremblay be buried in the sea for it was only proper because it was also the day of the Feast for Our Lady, Star of the Sea. It was said the British also sent some officers over to honor a fellow seaman.

Those in camp also surrendered when the British came sailing in. And the camp was burned down. The sailors were first taken to Vancouver Island and eventually from there sent back to France.

The events along the Pacific Northwest were soon forgotten by the world around them and dust binned into the annuals of history.

PART 3

With the Oregon question finally solved, between the US and Britain, the territory was largely left unorganized and not many settlers moved into the area. It wasn't until around 1850 or 1851 that the first known person moved into the bay where St. duTremblay declared it was part of France. It is doubtful that the person, known as Charles Oxford, knew this.

Oxford stayed in the area and traded with the local Indians. Records are unclear how long he stayed or when he died (and where). But his heirs can claim he was there first if nothing else.

It wasn't until around 1870 that the first records of a town began to appear concerning the area in question. It seems to have been called "Sheridan" as a number of former Union army men settled there with their families. Some became loggers, others various trades of the sea and the rest other needed trades. The name of the town survived for just over a decade.

With the town seeming to be growing when, in 1881, a massive forest fire raged through the area and even engulfed the town. The town didn't survive very well as it didn't have much to prevent fires or even save the town. So, it was mostly burnt down and many people either headed north towards Oregon City or south to various parts of California.

Those that stayed managed to struggle with whatever they could put together after the forest fire. But things started to change when, in 1885, a Frenchman, by the name of Jacques Brode appeared. He claimed he was a descendant of Charles Borde and wanted to see where the French once fought and lost to Britain.

Borde spoke decent English and was able to talk with the local townsfolks and showed them Charles Borde's log, which was kept as a family heirloom (and is now in the Oregon state museum), as well as telling them about the history of the area which they all appeared to know nothing about.

By 1888 Borde was still in the town but managed to convince them to change the name of the town. Naturally, it can be assumed, he wanted to name it after his ancestor but, fate had other ideas. The townspeople instead named it after Captain Guy St. duTremblay and immediately informed the Salem government of the change.

The change can be found in the records of the Oregon state archives.

Borde was greatly disappointed, and wrote in his journal about "those people who don't understand history or the honor of my family," but records state that he stayed on in the area, working on what appears to be a profitable maritime trading post for Asia and Alaska. Later, he became the town's mayor until his death many years later. He is buried in the local cemetery just up the hill from where my father is buried.

With the advent of the 20ᵗʰ century the town didn't grow that much. In fact, even when World War 1 happened the town did send its able-bodied men to war (and some never came back) but not much happened to the town and a malaise overcame it since it seems that the war over looked them and not much happened.

However, as the 20ᵗʰ century marched on it looked like the town would just be another small town that rose up and was forgotten by history. However, two things changed this direction: the Great Depression and the Dust Bowl.

It wasn't so much the Depression that effected the town. Rather, it was the starting the construction of US Route 101 and the town found out it was going to be connected to it. Since it was near the border with California the town was one of the first places that construction actually took place. Thus crews from around the state stayed in and around the town while construction took place in the area.

With the Dust Bowl people lost their farms, and livelihoods and so many of them packed up their belongings and headed west. While many headed for California a few went to Oregon and ended up supporting, directly or indirectly, the building of US Route 101. After the construction left the area, some followed the jobs while others stayed in the area and the town grew.

Also, the Civilian Conservation Corps was in the area expanding and improving various parks and logging roads that most people now just take for granted as always having been there.

In the late 1930s the US Navy looked at the area and its marginal maritime trade. With war already started in China and war clouds forming in Europe it was decided that the town's port would be ideal for protecting the US. Therefore, the port was upgraded to support small warships and an airbase was constructed for anti-submarine patrols (Because of the Navy's lack of anti-submarine aircraft the airbase was transferred to the US Army and they carried out the duties, at first, under the Army Air Forces and later its Antisubmarine Command.)

The naval port hosted destroyer escorts for both anti-submarine patrols as well as additional escorts for the various convoys that sailed up and down the west coast of the US. There was also Army coastal batteries to defend the port and town should any enemy ships appear[4].

With World War II ended the troops came home and the government had to decide what to do with all of its surplus equipment. For the city, the port and airport were transferred to the

---

[4] This was Battery Hunt. It was named after General Henry Hunt (September 14, 1819 – February 11, 1889) who was Chief of Artillery in the Army of the Potomac during the American Civil War. It was originally equipped with 2 -5 inch guns on both sides of the port entry (total of 4 guns).

county and state. The two battery emplacements were turned into city parks and hosts a great view of the Pacific Ocean. These abandoned battery positions were some of my favorite places to visit when I was young.

The airfield was converted to a regional airport with flights to Salem and Portland; as well as other places.

The old naval port was largely left untouched and was left to the elements and eventually to the homeless because the city could not afford such an expansion at a fast rate.

The construction of Interstate 5 nearly spelled the end of the town. With the interstate completed not many used US 101. Even people living in town were now able to cut their driving times down when they wanted to take a vacation to someplace like Eugene or Seattle. Many people moved out and not many moved back to replace them.

It was just near the end of the Vietnam War that the town received a cultural shock. With so many Vietnamese people fleeing their former country the US, and other nations, had to put them somewhere. One of the US places that were chosen was St. Tremblay. The government gave them many grants to help integrate the new arrivals.

The meeting of the two cultures must have shocked each other as neither side knew exactly what the other side wanted or needed. My parents arrived sometime before this and my father acted as liaison between the town and their soon to be new neighbors. He had served a number of years in the military and could pick up languages fairly easily.

Still, the town was in shock and didn't know what to do. My father attended some of the town council meetings and described them as "charged". Looking over the newspaper clipping, of that time, it must have been an understatement; many people were arrested or just packed their belongings and moved. He was able to convince them to renovate the old naval port as housing for the new arrivals.

He seemed to be the right man for the job because he was not only able to settle disputes from both cultures but also was able to recruit some in the town for help. Even with the untimely death of my mother my father stayed on long after his official job ended. He retired there and was something of a local legend.

Many of the townsfolks left because they didn't want to bother with this new cultural invasion. They sold their places, said goodbye to their neighbors and left for other places such as California or Portland. They never returned.

The newcomers didn't know much about their surrounding area so many of them stayed there and started to learn English, sent their children to school and bought many businesses that were now empty. This is why many of the businesses, especially around the port area, are Vietnamese.

With the close of the 20th century the town stabilized and what was once a great cultural divide was actually mended. Both sides came together and helped each other out. The town got use to Vietnamese style cooking and even built a monument to the brave Vietnamese who dared to leave their country and managed to make it to the United States. The original Vietnamese who landed there had children and started to explore their new homeland. Those that moved away often return for a visit and talk about the early days and how my father helped them settled in a new world.

How both sides survived when my father took holidays has always amazed me. Perhaps that is the time they started to realize that they needed to work together in order for both sides to survive and thrive.

With the coming of the 21st century the town decided to change its major industry; from doing some maritime trade to one of tourism. The town started with the water area by making a promenade where tourists could walk and businesses could cater to them.

Amidst the completion of the promenade area the town re-invented itself and started to advertise to the rest of the world. No longer was this a sleepy town that was waiting for death but was now a minor summer tourist attraction resort where people could either take a whale watching or fishing tours or go camping and fishing in the state park that surrounded the area.

The town has also become a sister city to the city of Trouville-sur-mer, France. In July you will see a combination of both US and French flags dotting along the main street. It is interesting to see Vietnamese businesses flying French flags and overcoming their own tragic history of their ancestor's former country.

EPILOGUE

If you go to St. Tremblay, Oregon today you should stop at the information center that stands alongside the promenade. There you will see a statue of Captain Guy St. duTremblay in his royal naval uniform and clutching a rosary in his hand; behind him you can read his story.

Except for the tourists many of those that do just stop and get some gas for their cars and a bite to eat for them and their families don't care about the history of this small town. While most don't even care about the town but you, dear reader, it is hoped that you will care and plan a visit. My father would like that as he and his wife were always entertaining everyone from townsfolks to government officials that came by and checked in on how things were going.

Now, my flight is being called and I'm going to where I once lived and visit my father and remember my mother.

THE BRIGADE

PROLOGUE

Have you ever been to Japan? To some the name conjures everything up from Samurais to sushi; and from geishas to Godzilla. But, to many Americans, it also brings up Commodore Matthew Perry's expedition and the changing of ideas. Ideas that evolved a certain way that ended with two atomic bombs being dropped on those ideas. Then the ideas were changed once again to the country of today.

It doesn't matter if you have been there or not for this is not a travel brochure. However, one of the more enduring images of Japan is the cherry blossom. People flock from around the Asian rim just to see the blossoms in bloom. But they often don't know the dark side of the blossoms.

When I graduated from university (thanks to the ROTC) I received orders to go to Japan. I had inherited my father's knack for learning languages and was ordered to Japan where I listened in on Chinese and Russian military communicates and then wrote up whatever I heard and tried to analyze it all. The job itself was interesting especially what I heard but can never tell the outside world.

Being one of the many new arrivals to Japan I soon made acquaintances with many other new placements from the various branches of service. The first thing we asked was "where you from" and then "why did you choose the military." Standard questions that got standard answers.

Beyond the standard chat we were able, on our days off, to explore Japan. At first it was mostly the local area but as we got more bolder, and I got to know the language a little more, we moved further and further away from the base.

We eventually made it to Osaka- twice. The first time we just visited the tourist sites and took in a few drinks and a few girls before heading back to base. I can't say it was anything special and I'm not sure why I we went back a second time some months later.

The second time was around cherry blossom season and my buddies convinced me to go back to Osaka and check out the local scenery (mostly the bars and girls). I wanted to do something a little different and we compromised.

One the second day in Osaka we took a bus and headed for Kuragari Pass which is east of the city. My father later talked about the time he was stationed in Hong Kong and flew to Japan on some business in Osaka and was shown the Pass. But he never said why he was there. Because of this mystery I wanted to go see it.

Kuragari Pass was once a major passage from Osaka to Nara. Now, it's just another hiking trail for the adventurous. When I was there not much was there and it was slowly being changed to a tourist hiking destination.

We got off the bus and started to look around. We found the standard temples and shrines dotting the landscape. However, one of the more interesting things, at least I, noticed, was that several people wore a silver cherry blossom on their lapel jacket. This was odd for a couple of reasons. One of which was who would wear a jacket in the middle of nowhere and second was why a silver cherry blossom.

I tried to ask the owners of the silver cherry blossom but all I got was a smile and something in Japanese that said they couldn't understand me.

I tried to ask some of the merchants in the area but all I got was a frightened look and was told not to talk or ask about those things. Just accept its presence and that's all. We were soon shown the bus stop back to Osaka and quickly left the area.

After leaving the service, and Japan, I finally got some answers. I now understand why the shopkeepers said nothing.

PART 1

It was during the period known as the Ishiyama Hongan-ji War (1570-1580) that the Kuragari Pass took importance with the silver cherry blossoms.

In mid-1573 nearly 200 warrior monks and commoners attacked, held and fortified the pass. They roamed the area freely and managed to defeat any endeavors that tried to force open the pass. It looked nearly hopeless as a key chokepoint was held.

In early 1574 a merchant known in legend as Tanaka went to one of the local temples around the town of Nara and prayed on what needed to be done to unlock the pass. He went home and the next day called upon the priests and told him what he dreamed of.

He said that he was walking in Kuragari Pass at night when he felt something hit his head. He looked down and found a cherry blossom on the pass. He knelt down to pick it up and study it better. However, more and more blossoms fell from the sky and covered the area.

As he further walked the path he noticed enemy soldiers were all dead and covered over with blossoms. Near the end of his trip a bright light from the sky shown down and a voice said, "Do this" and then all was dark and he was alone on the path. Not even a cherry blossom was left but neither were the soldiers.

The priests listened carefully and consulted among themselves. After much thought they pronounced and wrote in their books: *We have met with the merchant Tanaka and he has told us of his dream. After much prayer and consultation we have deemed it to be from the gods and worthy of their blessings.*

Tanaka then called all the people to the town square and told them what had happened. He must have been quite the talker as he whipped them into a war fervor and said the gods have blessed this undertaking. He then called for volunteers to break the barricade at Kuragari Pass. From far and near over 300 men, young and old, answered his call to arms.

They didn't have many modern weapons; mostly were equipped with farm tools and clubs. The cherry blossom was picked for their symbol and a dance and ritual were created in the belief that it would give them strength and an advantage in the coming battle.

Tanaka's command marched when he thought it was the right time and received the blessings of the gods. It was very early in the morning the cherry blossoms were in bloom along the pass and the wind was gently blowing. The successful attacked the first outpost mostly because of surprise and blunders from the defending force.

Awaken by hurried survivors the defenders of Kuragari Pass moved to their stations and waited for the attackers. They didn't have long to wait. In a period of just over two hours everyone of Tanaka's force were killed.

Tanaka was said to be one of the last ones to fall and the wind had picked up. It has been written that his compensation for this achievement was to see the cherry blossoms fall not on the enemy but on his own command. Then the sun rose and lit the pass.

The pass was held for a few more years until another, more organized and powerful, expedition forced open the pass. But no one remembered Tanaka.

In late 1931 the Japanese Kwantung Army based in China launched its campaign to expand Manchuria for Japan. It was this expansion that the need for a larger army, in China, appeared. Thus, a call for expanding its China presence started and one of the calls went to units in the Osaka Prefecture.

In 1935 a brigade was shipped from Osaka to China. This brigade was under the command of Major General Shim'ichi Gima, who was mid-aged, and was descendant of a minor Samurai.

Gima was the first commanding officer of the brigade. He trained the troops to have a loyalty to the Emperor and himself. While the brigade was officially called the "32nd Brigade (Osaka)" it would be more famous for its symbol- a silver cherry blossom and hence the legend of the Oka[5] Brigade was started.

In 1937 the Brigade was stationed along the Xar Moron River. When the Marco Polo Bridge incident occurred the Brigade was named the lead unit for the drive against the city of Zhangjiakou.

The Brigade encountered a few villages but found them to be empty. General Gima ordered the villages to be burned and continue to advance. The first village they found, with people, was

---

[5] Japanese for 'cherry blossom'

called Wangdong. It was a small village that wasn't militarily significant except that some Chinese soldiers stayed there for a few days and that it was in the zone of the Brigade's advance.

General Gima ordered all men and children to be executed and the women were left to his men. It has been said that many civilians were used as bayonet practice as well. Some of the men were used as a hunt and were chased by troops of the Brigade.

After the troops had their "fun" the women were also killed and the village burned. Nothing was left alive; not even the farm animals.

While the rape of Nanjing is justly recorded the actions against Zhangjiakou also deserve a mention. The countryside surrounding Zhangjiakou suffered heavily under the Brigade. Other units also joined in and it wasn't until nearly a week later that it was stopped by officers of the divisional command.

There is a shrine to the 32nd Brigade and it's in the Hongqilou Residential District of Zhangjiakou. There is a row of houses that now stands empty. They were commandeered by the 32nd Brigade for headquarters and "entertainment." It was here that a number of women were raped and beheaded. These houses are now considered to be haunted and no one had lived in them since the 1950s.

There are many stories of the 32nd Brigade as it marched south across China and they all seem to be about the same. One reoccurring item is that when replacements were brought to replace the troops killed or wounded they had to go through an initiation ritual. The ritual would end with the replacement cutting off the head or bayonetting of some helpless Chinese.

With the capture of Hong Kong, the Brigade was sent back, in September 1942, to Japan to relax. By this time the Brigade was decimated with various disease caused by constantly being on the march as well as suffering casualties. It needed a chance to recover and get ready for its next operation.

The convoy the Brigade was assigned to was attacked by the *USS Squid* which was on its first combat patrol. The *Squid* was later lost on this patrol but, according to post war reports, it did sink the merchant ship that Major General Shim'ichi Gima was assigned to. The *Squid* also received credit for sinking another merchant ship a few days earlier.

The Brigade stayed in Japan from late 1942 until it was deemed operational in mid-1944. It was smaller than what shipped out in 1935 with less than 4000 troops and now commanded by a Colonel Touma Ito who had seen action in the Philippines years early (including the Bataan Death March) and had risen up in the ranks. It was also assigned to the 85th Division at what could be considered familiar territory - Zhangjiakou.

While on garrison duty around Zhangjiakou the Brigade's main duty was to hunt down Chinese Communists guerrillas as well as their supporters. Over the time the Brigade was subjected to a number of ambushes and each time the number of troops available for patrol kept getting less and less.

It wasn't until late August 1945 that the Brigade saw action, but it was no longer major combat capable. For this was when the Soviet Union launched its attacked upon Japanese forces in Asia.

When the Battle of Zhangjiakou occurred, it wasn't much of a battle. Units of the Soviet Mongolian Cavalry Mechanized Group were able to breakthrough with ease and managed to capture most of the Japanese command around the Zhangjiakou region. The Japanese prisoners were sent back to the Soviet Union and the last were not released back to Japan until late 1946.

Before the surrender of the Brigade the senior officers committed ritual suicide. Colonel Ito was found wrapped up in the Brigade's flag and bullet to his head. It was the junior officers who did the surrender to Soviet forces.

Upon the surrender many people from the region told Soviet officials about the Brigade's involvement in the Zhangjiakou region many years before. Because of this, members of the Brigade were not accorded treatment as prisoners of war.

When the Brigade member returned to Japan, they found a different world from when they left it. Now, the Emperor was just a person and the American were now in control. Some members couldn't stand the strain of these changes, so they just gave up and killed themselves.

PART 3

In April 1952 the formal Allied occupation of Japan ended and Japan started to reclaim its sovereignty. However, the US was still able to maintain its bases there but didn't have time to keep Japan from any new problems because they were engaged in the war in Korea.

It was at this crossroad of Japanese history that, in the Osaka Prefecture, a group of former Imperial soldiers started dealing in prostitution for soldiers returning from Korea. From Japanese police records it appears these soldiers of the former Empire were mostly successful and were able to flourish in this time. Mostly because the police were still growing and didn't have the manpower, or training, to deal with everything.

More and more people were recruited to this new criminal organization and a new name was created- the Oka Brigade. Its symbol would be a silver cherry blossom.

By 1961 the Brigade had control of the Osaka Prefecture. Prostitution, blackmail and illegal drugs seem to be the mainstay of the group. It was also at this time it aroused the interest of the Yakuza and some type of merger was suggested.

The merger was rejected and a gang war started in 1962 for control of the Brigade. Assassinations, and other criminal activities against each other, were common and the police had their hands full trying to deal with both organizations and the growing body count around southern Japan.

It appears by mid-1964 a truce was called as the number of dead bodies went down to a more normal level. The Brigade never surrendered and was more firmly entrenched in the Osaka Prefecture. The Yakuza left them alone but continued to watch them.

With the end of the American war in Vietnam and the opening of China by President Richard Nixon the Brigade decided it was time to move international. After several attempts at establishing themselves outside Japan the Brigade finally was established itself in China. The Brigade started to establish itself, around 1976, in a familiar city- Zhangjiakou. From there they continued their "practices" and expanded into Mongolia and parts of the Soviet Union.

Within a few more years the Brigade moved southwards. They started to establish themselves in the Guangdong region and even into Hong Kong. With each attempt to establish itself the Brigade was met by opposition from already established criminal groups. Each attempt was faced the same way – gang wars that left the various cities bloodied but, in the end, the Brigade was able to find a niche for itself and the grudging respect of its rivals.

With the advent of the internet the Brigade added new "practices" to its growing portfolio; white collar and other activities allowed them to expand their networks and financial dealings.

Because the Brigade had a growing criminal influence in various cities a mounting concern creeped into various law enforcement agencies. Thus, during the Lunar New Year of 1995 Chinese, British and Japanese police assaulted various buildings that were controlled by the Brigade. The Chinese raided positions in both Guangdong and Zhangjiakou; the British stormed the Brigade's holdings in Hong Kong and the Japanese attacked their places in and around Osaka.

The raids of 1995 hurt the Brigade seriously. However, it didn't destroy it. Since that time the Brigade has rebuilt itself and re-established itself in various places.

Since the turn of the 21st Century the Brigade had changed its overt tactics for making money. They have bought several shops along Kuragari Pass and the surrounding area and owners are recognized by smart dress clothes and a silver cherry blossom pinned on their jacket lapels. From along the length of the Pass, tourists are used as laundering money operations and they innocently never know what is going on.

EPILOGUE

Over the course of the past few years I have been gathering documents from US, UK and Japanese government departments as well as their national archives about my father's duty in Hong Kong and how it dealt with the Cherry Blossom Brigade.

My father told me he had work in supplies while in Hong Kong. In truth he worked for the "Joint Allied Logistics Group" which was, at first, responsible for finding and servicing intelligent agents, in China, who survived both World War 2 and the Chinese Civil War.

Later, the Group was tasked with listening to Chinese communications once the agent lines went dead. Finally, they helped the French in their attempts to re-assert itself in what is now Vietnam.

Reports generation from the Group were sent out to various military commands. For American reports they first went to the United States Pacific Command and from there sent out to local commands concerning the material that was being dealt with.

I have seen several reports, highly redacted, that appears to mention Brigade's early attempted excursions into China.

From the US National Archives:

[date redacted]

[redacted] suggests Japanese [redacted] along southern China
coast.

From the UK National Archives:

[dated redacted]

Confirms [redacted] with Japanese. Suggest [redacted] as soon as
possible.

It is not clear from various UK reports if it says that a
contact in China is suggesting they do something or if it says that
the Allied command should do something

I have many reports that similar to these and while it is not
clear what exactly is going on it is clear that something is going on
even at a very low level. Especially in the early days of
Communist China. Perhaps the Brigade was trying to control
various Chinese government officials.

One document, from the Japanese National Police Agency
Security Bureau, written sometime in either the early 1960s which
said:

To:USPacCom

From: NPASB

Received latest information. We are interested in knowing more about activities in China. Request urgent meeting with main source.

It is not known what information they were responding from the US Pacific Command, but it must have raised warnings for an urgent meeting. Thus, my father was sent to Japan for meetings with his Japanese counterparts.

He stayed for nearly six months and had to leave the country in a hurry when he received a broken silver cherry blossom in the mail. He must have known what it meant and understood the warning. He had shown it to me once when I asked him about Japan. He didn't say anything, but his look told much. I never asked again.

If you meet anyone wearing a silver cherry blossom I would suggest you just smile and walk away. If you want to push your luck and know more about the symbol then I could not assure you of your safety. But then, who would believe you if you repeated such listened tales.

ABOUT THE AUTHOR

Guy Breshears was born and raised in Spokane, Washington, USA. He received both his BAE in Social Science Education and MA in History from Eastern Washington University in Cheney, Washington, USA. He is an educational professional and has taught at the primary and secondary levels both in the US and Hong Kong. With an interest in the advancement of knowledge, understanding and preservation of historical events and places he has lectured teachers and students about the importance of being appreciative of the past and why it is important to study and preserve it. He currently lives in Hong Kong with his wife and can often been seen walking around obscure places of Hong Kong looking for traces of history.